Laura Owen

Winnie
Says Cheese

OXFORD
UNIVERSITY PRESS

contents

Winnie's
One-Witch Band

Winnie
Says Cheese

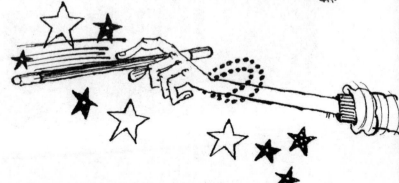

Winnie
and the Toof Fairy

Winnie and Wilbur were watching a wrestling match on telly and sharing a few snacks.

'Pull him over!' shouted Winnie at the telly. She jumped up from the sofa. 'Go on, grab him!' She shot out an arm to grab the air to show the wrestler how he should be doing it, but unfortunately Wilbur was in the way. **POW!**

'Mrrow!'

7

Wilbur's paw was over his mouth. There was a look of panic in his eyes.

'Oh, heck, Wilbur!' said Winnie. 'Have I punched all your teeth out?'

Wilbur slowly took his paws away from his mouth. He opened his mouth and felt for each tooth with his tongue. They were all still there.

'Thank stinky cheese for that!' said
Winnie. 'Shall I take you to Mr Drillikins
the dentist, just to check you over?'

'Mrow-ow-ow!' said Wilbur, hurrying
up the curtains to get out of reach.

'All right, all right!' said Winnie. 'But you be careful. Those teeth might be loose. You suck a nice warm-worm and frogspawn smoothie through a straw. I'll finish off the nibbles by myself.'

Winnie settled back on the sofa.

'Trip him up! Pull his hair!' she shouted while she dipped an elephant's toenail into stinkwort sauce and popped it into her mouth. Chew-chew. 'Tickle him!' she screamed as she took a liquorice rat's tail and began to chew-chew-chew on that.

But, suddenly, 'Mnnn!' mumbled Winnie, her hand to her mouth. She stuck long fingers into her mouth and pulled out . . .

10

'A toof!'

'Meeow!' said Wilbur, looking with interest.

'What am I going to do without thith toof?' asked Winnie, holding it up. 'I need thith toof! I can't talk properly wivout it! I'll look like one of them wrethlerth on the telly! I'll never be beautiful again! And I'll thtarve to death. What'th that?'

Wilbur was nudging Winnie, offering her his straw.

'No!' wailed Winnie. 'I don't want thmoothies thucked through a thtraw!' But Wilbur had grabbed hold of the telephone book and was pointing at a phone number. 'NO, no, no!' wailed Winnie, even louder. 'I'm not going to Mr Drillikinth! Never!'

13

But Wilbur had one more helpful hint to try. He was pirouetting on his toes, his arms curved above his head and a soppy look on his face.

'What on erf?' asked Winnie. Then she got it. 'Oh, I know! You're being a fairy!' Wilbur nodded enthusiastically. 'Of courth!' said Winnie. 'I can leave my toof for the toof fairy and get a wifth from her in ecthchange for the toof. Oooo, what thall I chooth for my wifth, Wilbur?'

Actually, choosing her wish was easy. There was one thing more than any other that Winnie wanted just then.

'I mutht write a note to tell the fairy my wifth,' said Winnie. 'Where'th my pen, Wilbur?'

15

Winnie scrawled with her pen.

'There! Lookth good, doethn't it!'

Wilbur curled a lip and shook his head.

'Oh, thtop looking at me like that, cat!'
said Winnie. 'You know I'm not very
good at writing. I jutht thought a fairy
might underthtand. Will you write it for
me, pleathe, Wilbur?'

Wilbur did write it, in his best paw-
writing. He wrote it very tiny and just
right for a fairy. It said:

Please give Winnie
a new tooth
Thank you.
W & W

'Thweet dreamth, Wilbur,' said Winnie.

Winnie was woken in the night by
something tickling around her face.

'Atithoo!' sneezed Winnie. Then, 'Poo!'
she shouted. 'What'th that 'orrible
thmell?' Then she sank back into snoring,
Snooore, phiew, snooore, phiew.

The little-wittle tooth fairy smelt of
summer breezes wafting over dew-fresh
meadow flowers sprinkled with icing sugar
and love. Nobody had ever said 'poo' to her
before. She put her tiny fists on her teeny
pink waist. She stomped weeny green-
slippered feet across Winnie's pillow.

She grabbed hold of a titchy handful of
Winnie's tangle of hair, and heaved herself
up onto Winnie's cheesy-white cheek.
Then she took her wincy little wand and—
WHACK!—she walloped it hard onto
Winnie's great snoring mountain of a nose.
'Eh? What?' said Winnie, sitting up.

The fairy tumbled, but she flapped her
incy-wincy mauve wings to flutter to
where the tooth and the note were waiting
for her.

The tooth fairy held her meeny-miny-
mo wand to glow over the note, and she
read Winnie's wish. And a minuscule
wicked grin came on to her fairy face.
Zip-zap went the wincy yellow wand
and—

Gulp! 'Eh, what was that?' said Winnie, feeling for her mouth. 'Hey, Wilbur! Guess what? I've got my new tooth! I can say, "Six silly slugs sat sipping sausage syrup through straws!" My wish has come true! Here, let me have a look!'

Winnie jumped out of bed and grabbed her wand.

'Abracadabra!'

Instantly the candles were lit and a mirror was gleaming with a come-hither look. Winnie arranged herself into a charming pose in front of the mirror. Then she smiled, and . . . oh, dear.

'Mrrow-hissss!' Wilbur scrabbled under the bed covers.

'Oh, heck!' cried Winnie as she saw

herself. 'Whatever has that blooming fairy done? She's given me a fearful fang! I look a right fright!'

23

Winnie's eyes were darting here and
there, looking for a fairy twinkle . . . and
she spotted it, still on her pillow.

'There it is!' shouted Winnie. She
swung her wand to swat it,
Abracadabra!

Instantly the twinkle around the fairy
was replaced by a buzz of midges around
the fairy.

But ... **zip-zap** went the tiddly
tooth fairy wand. And instantly Winnie
was covered in warts.

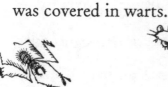

'*Abracadabra!*'

The fairy smelt of manure.

Zip-zap!

Winnie's skin turned blue.

'*Abra—*'

'MMEEEEOOWWW!' interrupted
Wilbur. He'd poked his head out from the
covers and found something nestling
under the pillow. It was something as tall
as the tooth fairy and not perhaps quite as
white as it might be, but Wilbur knew just
what it was and where it was needed. He
held it out to Winnie.

'My tooth!' said Winnie. 'My very own
dear tooth! Oh, *Abracadabra!*'

And instantly Winnie's own tooth was
back in her head, and the fang and the
warts and blue had all gone. And so had
the tooth fairy.

'Well,' said Winnie as she snuggled back into bed. 'That just goes to show, doesn't it?'

'Meow?' asked Wilbur.

'It shows that if you want a wish doing, you'd better just blooming well do the wish yourself,' said Winnie.

'Meeow,' agreed Wilbur.

Itchy Witchy

Winnie held the telling-moan away from her ear and winced at big sister Wanda's voice.

'Are you listening, Winnie?' screeched Wanda. 'The witches' cat show is tomorrow. I'm putting Wayne in for it, of course. He won it last year, you know. I've just had his teeth whitened. And highlights put in his fur.'

Wayne was Wanda's snooty sleek-as-a-panther cat.

29

'Have you still got that scraggy old catty thing of yours?' asked Wanda. 'What was he called?'

'He's called Wilbur,' said Winnie. 'And he's lovely.'

'Well, we'll all see just how lovely he is at the show, won't we! He hee!' laughed Wanda.

'No,' said Winnie. 'I wasn't going to—'

'He hee! He hee!' cackled Wanda. 'I
knew it! I said to Wayne, I said, "I bet
Winnie won't dare to put that Wilbur in
for the show because she knows very well
he'll come bottom of the whole thing!"
He heee! I just knew it!'

31

Winnie glared at the telling-moan. 'Well, you knew wrong, Wanda the Witch!' she said. 'The only bottom thing at the show will be your Wayne winning the competition for the cat who has the witch with the biggest bottom—YOURS! Wilbur *will* be in the show, and he might just win it! So there!'

Winnie slammed down the telling-moan. Then she chewed a nail. 'Oh, banana bandages!' she said to herself. 'Winnie the Witch, whatever have you gone and done now?'

33

Winnie looked at Wilbur lying happily in the sun. There was a spider's web stuck between Wilbur's ears. There was a bald patch on his back where he'd rolled around on hot tar and it had pulled some of his fur off. There was some pond slime hanging from his tail. And flies were hovering over him in a way that suggested that he might not be smelling very fresh at the moment.

Winnie found a pair of shark-fin scissors, some carpet shampoo, a big bottle of skunk scent, a brush, a comb, some slug-slime hair gel, some gizzard glue and a ball of black wool, and she took them all outside.

'Oh, Wilbur!' she called.

Wilbur opened one eye.

'Come to Winnie, Wilbur!' called
Winnie.

Wilbur's ears went flat onto his head.
Up he leapt, and he was about to run
when—

'*Abracadabra!*' went Winnie, and
instantly poor Wilbur was frozen still.
'I'm sorry about this, Wilbur, but I've got
to make you beautiful,' said Winnie.

Winnie got to work, washing . . . and
combing . . . and sticking wool over bald
bits. And then she saw a little something
hop-hop-HOP in Wilbur's fur.

'Oh, heck, Wilbur, you've got fleas!' said Winnie. She caught the flea mid-hop and popped it into her mouth. 'Mmm,' she said. 'Quite tasty in a tickle-your-taste-buds kind of way, but I don't think they give you a prize at the show if you've got fleas. Come on, Wilbur. We're off to the vet's to get you some flea treatment,' said Winnie.

Winnie un-froze Wilbur once he was inside the carrying box. It's horrible being in a box. There's nowhere to hide. Wilbur felt the jolting and swaying as Winnie got off her broomstick and carried the box into the surgery. Then he smelt that vetty smell.

'Meeeeooooowww!' he wailed miserably.

'My goodness,' said the vet. 'When did this animal last see a vet?'

'Oh, ages ago,' said Winnie. 'He hates vets.'

'Mrrrow!' went Wilbur, then he showed just how much he hated vets by scrabbling up this one and sitting on his head. He took off the vet's toupee when Winnie lifted him down.

'Is that an animal that went up and died there?' asked Winnie.

40

41

The vet squirted stuff on to Wilbur to get rid of the fleas. The fleas march-hopped—cough, sneeze!—down off Wilbur and on to Winnie and the vet. Itch-itch, scratch.

'Now,' said the vet. Itch, scratch. 'This cat needs injections for cat flu and cat cold and cat sore-throat and cat ingrowing toenails and cat tennis elbow.'

'Are you sure?' said Winnie. 'How much will that lot cost?'

'Let me see,' said the vet, and he began poking numbers into his calculator. **Itch, scratch.** Winnie saw a number getting longer and longer.

'Quick, Wilbur!' she whispered. 'Let's go!'

Wilbur did look very smart at the show, even if he didn't look happy. Winnie felt worried and **itch-itch** scratchy.

But Wanda and Wayne were smug-as-a-bug happy. Wayne lounged in a suave and sophisticated smiley way.

44

'What do you think of my Wayne, then, Winnie? Just feel how silky his fur is. Go on, Win, have a feel!' said Wanda.

So Winnie reached out a hand to feel how soft Wayne was. And as she touched him . . . this hopped . . . and that hopped . . . and those hopped . . . off Winnie and on to Wayne. **Itch-itch, scratch. Itch-itch-itch, scritchety-scratch.**

'Oo, here comes the judge!' said Wanda.

'Just watch what he says about Wayne and Wilbur, he hee!' *Itch-scratch,* went Wayne. 'Don't do that, Wayne darling,' said Wanda. 'Be nice for the judge.'

The judge poked at Wilbur first.

'Mrrrow!' went Wilbur. He'd had enough of being poked for one day.

The judge lifted Wilbur's tail.

'Hisss!' Scratch! went Wilbur.

'Disqualified!' said the judge.

'He heee!' said Wanda.

The judge poked at Wayne.

'Purrrr!' went Wayne.

The judge lifted Wayne's tail.

'Purrr!' Smarm! went Wayne.

'Very nice indeed,' said the judge.

But just then—**itch**, went Wayne.
Itch-itch, scratch-scratch. And
then the judge felt an itch and began to
scratch.

'Uh!' he shouted, snatching his hands
away from Wayne. 'This cat has got
FLEAS!'

He was about to disqualify Wayne, but there was no need to because everybody was disqualifying themselves, running and shoving to get away from the fleas and the show.

'What a lot of fuss over a few fleas!' said Winnie, happily scratching herself. 'Call themselves witches! Huh! Come on, let's go home, Wilbur.'

Back home Wilbur rolled in the grass to get himself back to himself.

'Here's a rosette for you!' said Winnie, and she fixed a dried tarantula to his ear. 'It's for being the best cat for me!'

'Purrr!' said Wilbur proudly.

They sat and ate squashed-flea biscuits. And all the fleas that had fled to Winnie's head, hopped back on to Wilbur because Wilbur tasted nicer, if you were a flea.

And so all the fleas were back home, too.
Except for one adventurous flea who had
hopped on to Wayne and then on to Wanda
because he liked the taste of her hair spray.
So Wanda was going **itch-itch,
scritchety-scratch.**

Hee heee!

Winnie's One-Witch Band

Winnie was just pegging out her washing when she heard music coming from the village. Winnie stopped still, a pair of bloomers held up in the air, and she listened.

'Who can it be?' Winnie asked Wilbur. 'It sounds the way my tummy sounds after I've eaten one of your snake sausage and chilli stews then drunk a fizz-pop pond cordial sucked through a straw,' said Winnie.

'Except that this sound is less gurgly.
Let's go and find out where it's coming
from!'

So Winnie and Wilbur went down into
the village, and they found the sound
coming from the library.

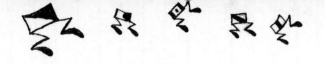

'They're all singing!' said Winnie, as she peeped through the window.

'La la laaa!' warbled the ladies' high-up voices. 'Bom boom-boom-bum,' sang the low-down men's voices. 'Traliddle-traloddle,' they all sang together. 'Tra . . .

AHHHH!' they shrieked as they suddenly saw Winnie's and Wilbur's faces squashed against the glass.

'Why ever have they stopped?' asked Winnie. She soon found out why.

The conductor came to the library door.

'Go away!' he said. 'You're frightening my choir and spoiling my rehearsal! We have a concert to prepare!'

'What concert?' asked Winnie.

'The library concert,' said the conductor. 'To raise money to buy more books for the library.'

'And who's in the choir?' asked Winnie.

'Anybody who wants to sing,' said the conductor.

'Ooooo, goody-goody!' said Winnie,
pushing her way into the library. 'Where do
I stand?'

'Well,' said the conductor, looking worried.
'Um . . . what kind of voice do you have?'

'A good loud one!' said Winnie.

'No, no,' said the conductor, flapping his
hands like a baby bird. 'What I meant was,
do you have a low voice or a high voice?'

'Oh, I can go up and down like a kangaroo in a lift!' said Winnie.

'Perhaps I'd better try you out,' said the conductor wearily. He sat down at a piano and played—**plink-plonk-plink-plonk-plink-plonk-plink**—up and down. 'Now, sing that back to me, please,' he told Winnie.

Winnie opened her mouth and—

croak-moan-honk-screechety-croak—down and up, sang Winnie.

Wilbur had his paws over his ears. The choir winced. The conductor had gone pale. 'Er . . . ' he said. 'I don't think we can use you in our choir, Winnie.'

'Why not?' asked Winnie. 'Wasn't I loud enough? I can go louder. Listen!'

60

CROAK-MOAN-HONK-
SCREECHETY-CROAK!

Books fell from the shelves all around.
The flowers in the vase wilted. Mice ran for
their holes. Bookworms buried themselves
deep into the fattest volumes they could
find. And the choir all fainted—**thunk!**

61

'Er . . . no,' said the conductor weakly holding on to a bookcase. 'I'm afraid that really wasn't good enough.'

'Oh,' said Winnie. 'So you don't want me?'

The conductor shook his head.

There was silence for a moment, then . . . 'Ooo, but I've got a good idea!' said Winnie. 'My cat, Wilbur, he's got a lovely voice. You listen to him!'

'Must I?' said the conductor.

'Go on, Wilbur!' said Winnie.

Wilbur looked bashful. His toes turned in, he looked at the floor with a silly grin on his face, and shook his head.

'Go ON, Wilbur!' urged Winnie.

Wilbur meow-giggled.

But then he sat up straight and opened
his mouth and everyone in the choir
covered their ears.

But what came out of Wilbur's mouth was beautiful. 'Meeeeoow! Mew-mew-mew, miow-wow!'

As Wilbur sang, the choir took their hands from their ears and joined in.

'Oh!' said the conductor, clasping his hands together. 'Oh, Wilbur, that was *dee-vine!*' Then the conductor frowned. 'But won't it look rather odd if we have a cat in our choir?'

'Oh-oh, I know what we can do!' said
Winnie, jumping around in excitement.

'If I wear a long skirt, then Wilbur can
hide under it and sing and I'll just open and
close my mouth and everybody will think
it's me who is singing. It'll look quite
normal! I'll show you how. Sing, Wilbur!'

Wilbur sang—'Meeeeoow! Mew-mew-
mew, miow-wow!'—while Winnie silently
opened and closed her mouth and waggled
her eyebrows. She waved her hands
expressively, knocking the few books left
on shelves—**thump thumpety-
thump**—onto the floor.

'Good, wasn't it?' said Winnie, when they'd
finished. 'Shall I go and find a long skirt?'

'Er . . . no,' said the conductor. 'I have a
better solution! Wilbur can be our soloist!
He can perform *with* the choir while not
being part *of* the choir. Would that suit you,
Wilbur? Do you have your own bow tie?'

Giggle, went Wilbur. 'Meow.' And he put
a paw to his mouth and pretended to be
embarrassed.

'Show off!' said Winnie.

The conductor pointed his baton at
Winnie. 'You had better go!'

67

So Winnie went, stamping her feet crossly

stomp-stomp

like a drum—out of the library. She went

home and cooked herself some tea

crash! bang! clang!

went the pots and pans,

sounding like cymbals.

Winnie took her tea out into the garden.

Tweet-tweet,

like a pipe, went a little bird.

68

Hoot,

like an organ, went an owl.

Winnie stopped eating and listened.

Croak-croak-belch,

like no musical instrument

ever invented, went a toad.

'That has given me a brillaramaroodle

idea!' said Winnie suddenly. 'Where's my

wand, Wilbur?' But Wilbur wasn't there.

'Oh, I'll get it myself,' said Winnie.

Then she waved it, *Abracadabra!*

In an instant, Winnie was outside the library, covered in sounds. She had hooting owls of different sizes on her shoulders and head. She had a toad in her pocket which could be squeezed for a croak. She had a rat in another pocket with a tail hanging out to be pulled when she wanted a squeal. She had saucepan-lid cymbals strapped to her knees, and clackety clogs on her feet.

'I'm a one-witch band!' she said, and the wand conducted, all on its own.

Crash-clang-croak-squeak, hoot-hoot-hoot-hoot-ping!

That last ping wasn't really part of the music. It was the elastic going on Winnie's knickers.

Inside the library, Wilbur and the choir
were performing to people who had
bought tickets.

'Meeeoww! Tra-la-la-la-la, boom-
boom-boom!'

Outside the library, Winnie played
while the children gathered to hear and
cheer her. And when the choir concert
finished, Wilbur came outside and joined
Winnie.

'Abracadabra!'

Instantly, Wilbur had clogs on his
paws, and all the right moves. Wilbur tap-
danced to Winnie's band. He held out her
hat and collected lots more money for the
library. And everybody danced.

As they—**clank-crash-croak
tappety-tap-parp-whoops!**—
walked home in the moonlight, Winnie
said to Wilbur, 'Life is a kind of music,
when you think about it.'

'Meeow,' agreed Wilbur happily.

Winnie Says Cheese

'Oo, look at little you with your pink nose
and fluffy-wuffy coat!' said Winnie,
showing Wilbur a photo in an album. 'You
were such a sweet 'ickle kitten in those days!'

Wilbur smiled and rubbed his face
against Winnie. He gazed up at her.
'Purrr!'

Winnie had a soppy look on her face.
'Do you know,' she said, 'I remember the
day I chose teeny little Wilbur out of all

75

those little fluff-ball kittens in the cave. I
chose you instead of any of those others
because . . .' Winnie's face changed. 'Oh,
yes, you dug your claws into my cardigan
and you wouldn't let go and the goblin
grabbed my broom and wouldn't give it
back until I paid for you and promised to
take you away.'

'Mrrow!'

'Oh, but you were as cute as a newt in those days, Wilbur!' Winnie sniffed. 'Of course you've grown big and shaggy and smelly since then.' Winnie looked at the wet patch on her sleeve where Wilbur had drooled. 'And a bit disgusting, if you don't mind me saying so, Wilbur.'

Wilbur did mind her saying so. Wilbur
turned the pages of the album until he
came to some photos of Winnie when she
was a titchy little witchy girl. Wilbur
nudged Winnie to show that he thought
that she was sweet when she was little too.
And she was. Little Winifred Witch had
gappy teeth in a plump face and lots of
frizzy black hair.

'Ah!' said Winnie. But Wilbur hadn't finished. He kept turning the pages, and Winnie saw herself growing older and stringier and tattier and more wrinkly with each one.

'Oh, where's my wand, Wilbur?' shouted Winnie. 'I can soon sort this.' She pointed the wand at her face. *'Abracadabra!'* She pointed it at her hair. *'Abracadabra!'*

The next instant Winnie didn't look
like Winnie any more. Winnie fingered her
face and her hair.

'It feels funny,' she said. She could
hardly move her mouth because her skin
was so tight. 'It's as smooth and soft as an
eel's eyeball. Am I beautiful, Wilbur?'

'Hisss!'

'Let's have a look see,' said Winnie, and
she marched over to the mirror in the hall.

'AAAAH! Ooo, no!' said Winnie,
clutching her face. 'It's Mask Woman!
That's not me! Ooo, quick, get me back
to being real, even if real does mean
wrinkles! *Abracadabra!*'

And real Winnie was back again, but still frowning at the mirror. 'Mouldy maggots, I've just realized something!' she said. 'Look at that!'

Winnie grabbed a photo. 'Mildewed midges, Wilbur! I'm wearing exactly the same outfit now as I was then, and that photo was taken umpteen years ago! It's time I changed what I wear, even if I don't change me! I want some smart new photos for the album.'

So Winnie looked for witch clothes on the internet.

'I'll have one of those!' said Winnie. 'Ooo, and them in the orange with silver trimmings! And I'd look a treat in that one!'

Click, click went Winnie, then she scowled. 'What size am I, Wilbur? Oh, heck, I can't be doing with all this. Pass my wand over!' Winnie zapped the computer screen with her wand. *Abracadabra!*'

Instantly there appeared one of these . . .
and two of those . . . and some of them . . .

'I'm going to try them all on!' said
Winnie.

Winnie stripped down. She pulled on the
hot pants.

Wilbur sniggered into a paw.

'My legs look like twiglets!' said Winnie.
'What would cover them up?'

Winnie pulled the ball gown over her
head and let it cascade down her.

'Oo, this feels as gorgeous as a trifle
surprise with creamed worm topping!'

Wilbur spun his paw, so Winnie did a
twirl to make the skirt stick out. But she
twirled a bit too fast.

'Oooer, I've come over all dizzy!'

CRASH!

Winnie fell on her bum, her twiglet legs in the air.

'Did I look like Cinderella?' Winnie asked Wilbur as she got herself up. Wilbur made a face. 'More like an ugly sister, I suppose,' said Winnie. 'Botherarmarations. Nothing really suits, does it?'

Winnie put her fists to her skinny hips. 'I wish I was like you, Wilbur,' she said. 'You wear the same old black fur every blooming day, and it somehow looks just right.' Then Winnie brightened. 'Hey, that's a thought, Wilbur! Why don't I try black fur like yours?' Winnie snatched up her wand, just as there was a thumping at the front door. *Abracadabra!* shouted Winnie.

Instantly, there was Winnie, dressed top to toe in a kind of black furry hooded Babygro with added ears and a tail.

'Lovely and warm!' said Winnie, admiring and stroking herself in the mirror and giving her tail a twirl before she hurried to answer the door.

Thump, screech, creeeeak!

Winnie opened the door and . . .

'Wooof woof woof yap-yappety yap!'

Wilbur watched in amazement as
Winnie shot back into the house, closely
followed by the dog from next door that
was snip-snapping at her tail.

'Wilbur, HEEEELLLLPPPP!'
shouted Winnie.

89

'Scruff!' called the voice of Jerry, Winnie's giant neighbour. 'Bad boy, come back, Scruff!' Jerry folded himself over at the waist so that he could fit into Winnie's house. 'I'm ever so sorry about him, missus!' said Jerry. 'Scruff!'

Winnie had clambered on to the top of the dresser and was balanced there, but the dresser was swaying. The plates on it were swaying too.

'Grrrrr!' said Scruff.

'He don't know who you are, looking like that, missus! He's only being a good guard dog,' said Jerry.

'Well, I don't want to be blooming guarded!' said Winnie, grasping her tail to get it out of dog-teeth reach.

Jerry scratched his head. 'Why are you dressed like that, missus, if you don't mind me asking?'

'Grrrr-yap!' Scruff jumped up, his paws on the dresser.

'Oooer!' wailed Winnie as the dresser began to tip in slow motion, plates falling and smashing one by one. Winnie was falling too. 'Because . . .' **Smash!** 'I wanted . . .' **Smash!** 'to look . . .' **Smash-smash!** 'DIFFERENT!' **Smash-smash-smash!**

Winnie landed in the pile of broken crockery. For a moment there was stillness and silence.

Then Winnie pushed back her hood.

'YAP-ya—oh!' said Scruff, and his tail went between his legs.

Winnie sat amongst the mess, but suddenly she smiled. Then she cackled with laughter.

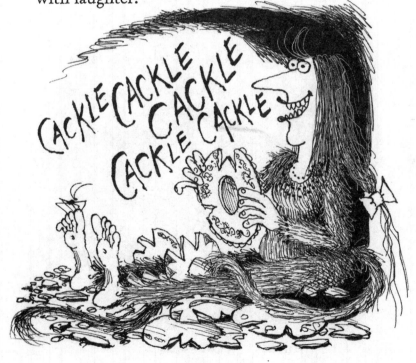

CACKLE CACKLE CACKLE CACKLE CACKLE CACKLE CACKLE

93

'Well, I suppose I do look different,
don't I? Fetch the camera, Wilbur!
Cheddar-Lancashire-Red Leicester-
Wymeswold-Stilton . . . hurry up, Wilbur!
. . . Double Gloucester-Stinking Bishop-
Cheshire-Wensleydale-CHEESE!'

Click! went Wilbur.

'Your turn now!' said Winnie. So
Wilbur stuck Winnie's hat on his head,
and grinned his best grin.

'Mrreee-ow!'

Click! went Winnie. Then **Click! Click!** because Jerry's and Scruff's faces looked so funny and she wanted them in the album too. 'There,' she said. 'Plenty of new photos, and every one of them as daft as a knotted noodle. Now, what shall we do?'

'Play frisbee?' suggested Jerry.

'With all these cracked plates!' said Winnie. 'Good idea!'

So they went and played in the garden, and had a smashing time.